Tiny Tin Elf

by Eric G Müller

illustrated by Ella Manor Lapointe

ALKION PRESS

For Sebastian and Anika

This edition first published in 2020 by Alkion Press
14 Old Wagon Road, Ghent, NY, 12075
Alkion-Press.com
ISBN: 978-1-7340170-4-5
Printed in the USA

Tiny Tin Elf

by Eric G Müller

illustrated by Ella Manor Lapointe

Every time Gracie went to visit her grandfather during the winter, he allowed her to put three shovels of coal into the big black stove. Grandpa, who lived alone on his farm, would open up the ornate door of the cast iron stove, stoke the fire with a poker and say, "Look sweetie, the fire is hungry for its fodder," which always made Gracie giggle. Then she'd take the shovel with the long handle, sink it into the chestnut size chunks of coal, and throw them quickly into the stove, taking care not to burn her fingers.

One cold and snowy afternoon, Gracie decided to put more coals on the fire, without waiting for Grandpa, who was chopping wood outside. The red-hot coals hissed as she opened the cast iron door, and the heat from the stove rushed to her face. She stepped back, clutched the shovel with determination, and shoved it deep into the coal bucket. Using both her hands she lifted the load and was about to cast the coals into the curling flames when a thin voice peeped, "Stop! Oh, please don't!" Gracie looked down and saw a tiny tin elf, half buried in the coals. She recognized it as one of the six winged elves that hung from the freely moving mobile above Grandpa's rocking chair next to the coal stove. She glanced up and saw that one was missing.

"Oh, poor thing, I almost threw you into the fire." Gracie put the shovel back into the bucket, closed the stove door, and carefully lifted the elf from the coals.

"Thank you for not throwing me into the flames. You are kind and you can call me Flinley."

"Pleased to meet you, Flinley." Gracie wiped and blew the black coal dust from the elf's face and wings just as Grandpa entered, his cap, beard, and coat sprinkled with a white layer of fluffy snowflakes.

"Grandpa, can you please fasten this tin elf back onto the mobile? The poor thing fell into the coal bucket." Gracie handed him the tin elf.

"Fell into the coal bucket, eh? Well, well, that certainly is no place for any elf of the air... unless he was trying to tell you something. They do that sometimes. But don't you worry, we'll get the elf flying and dancing again in a jiffy." Gracie liked it when Grandpa used words like 'jiffy.'

Grandpa removed his cap and coat and tossed them over the coat rack, causing the snow to scatter all about. He stepped into the living room and took the tiny tin elf into his big strong hands. Gently he bent the wings back into shape and hung it up with the other elves. "There you go," and he tapped the mobile so that all six tin elves swayed happily to and fro. Tipsy, the black cat with the white-tipped tail purred and rubbed herself against Grandpa's leg.

The next morning Gracie went outside to build a snowman. The sun shone and she sang a happy song as she rolled, stacked and patted the snow into shape. She gave the snowman a smiley face with two chunks of coal for the eyes, a crooked carrot for the nose, and a curved stick for the mouth.

As Gracie plonked an old straw hat onto the snowman's big round pate, she heard a cheerful voice chirp, "Hello there, it's me, Flinley." The elf she had saved from the fire flew down and sat on the end of the carrot.

"Oh, it's you," and Gracie clapped her hands in delight.

"Flinley it is!"

"How can you fly around like that?"

"Flinley can fly wherever Flinley chooses. The swinging mobile is my home, just like Grandpa's house is his home. I come and go as I please."

"Were you trying to tell me something yesterday when you fell into the coal bucket?"

"Yes, yes, for a while already, but you never looked or listened. Besides, had I not fallen into the bucket you might have burned yourself."

"So, I should really be thanking you."

"Enough of this silly-sally-billy-bally-chitter-chatter; Flinley wants to show you something. Now! So, come along," and he spread his pretty wings and flew toward the big red barn behind Grandpa's house. He flitted through a chink in the wall and disappeared. The heavy wooden door creaked loudly as Gracie pushed it open. The barn smelled of hay and it was dark and bare, except for some pigeons that fluttered up in the rafters. At one time Grandpa had kept cows, horses, goats, some sheep, and chickens, but that was many years ago and the stalls, coops

and pens were empty now. Save for Tipsy, the cat, he no longer kept any animals.

"Flinley, where are you?" she called. Gracie had never been in the barn alone before, and she felt a little afraid.

"Right here, swimming in a warm sunbeam." Flinley, joined by a host of graceful fairies, dove in and out of a shaft of light that shone through a small window. Their runic dance looked like flower blossoms, shifting and changing colors as they wove in and out of the light. Gracie laughed, which made Flinley and his fairy friends dance more boisterously. "Oh, but I am forgetting myself," the elf twittered, slowing down. "I came here to show you something special." Flinley hovered in the middle of the sunbeam, his wings moving almost as fast as a hummingbird's. "Something very specific. Something very important. Something secret. Something that needs to be revealed." Flinley bade the fairies farewell, did a loop de loop, and landed on Gracie's hand. "But first, Flinley will introduce you to Keynotteroom."

"Who is Keynotteroom?" Gracie asked, but Flinley had already dashed off and disappeared behind three hay bales at the back of the barn. Gracie found Flinley waiting on a large tree stump next to a narrow and steep staircase. Gracie had never seen these stairs before. Flinley bent over the wide old oak stump, which was firmly rooted into the ground, cupped his hands, and called down into a large crack, "Keynotteroom, come out. There is someone I want you to meet."

The oak stump creaked, the crack widened, and a short stocky dwarf stepped out. He had mossy eyebrows, a tangled bushy beard, and he wore an acorn hat on his head. His fingers looked like root-stubbles and his nose jutted out like a bulbous knot on a tree. As he yawned and stretched, he grew in size and his whole body creaked and cracked.

"Is she the one to make him laugh again?"

"She is indeed," Flinley answered. "Meet Gracie."

"Good. We have waited long enough for you." He looked straight up at Gracie with his deep-set eyes that gleamed like polished gemstones, and saluted her. "I am Keynotteroom, guardian of all the keys, locks, bolts, handles, latches, levers, knobs, switches, and padlocks on this old farm." He hopped onto the tree stump, looking bulky and rough next to the little winged elf. With legs astride he asked, "Are you willing to undertake the task?"

Gracie swallowed. "I-I-I... don't know... what task?"

"You do not know?" Keynotteroom asked in a gruff voice, his brow wrinkling into tiny furrows. "Hasn't Flinley told you? It should be obvious."

"Let's rather show her. Then she'll understand." Flinley flew onto Gracie's shoulder, stroked her cheek, and whispered into her ear, "Don't mind his rough and rugged ways. He is really very kind and means well."

"What are you waiting for? Let's get a move on." Keynotteroom jumped off the tree stump and bounded up the narrow stairs. Flinley flew after him, and Gracie trailed behind. At the top of the stairs Keynotteroom ordered, "Reach for the key that is on the ledge above the door." Gracie stepped onto a wooden box, stood on her tippy toes, felt for the large key, and brought it down. "Now unlock the door and push it open." She did as she was told and all three entered the hayloft at the back of

the barn, in which she had never set foot before. She gasped at what she saw.

Instruments from around the world filled the entire loft. Guitars, mandolins, banjos, violins, violas, balalaikas, lutes, and many more stringed instruments hung from the rafters. On the floor and stacked against the walls, were drums, xylophones, harps, lyres, gongs and a big double bass. Neatly arranged on various shelves were flutes, clarinets, an oboe, pipes, whistles, horns, castanets, rattles and shakers. From another rafter hung a row of brass instruments: a trumpet, saxophone, cornet, French horn, bugle, trombone and a big tuba. But there were also many instruments from far away countries that she had never seen before, and she wondered what they were called and what they sounded like. She walked around this wonderland of instruments, stopping here and there, filled with awe. In the far corner she spotted a beautiful cello, especially made for a child her age. Though it was covered with a thick layer of dust, she sighed and thought, *Ah, if only I could play the cello.* Eventually, she asked: "What are all these instruments doing here?"

"Your grandfather collected and played them all," Flinley said, settling on top of a harp." In the evenings, after a hard day's work, Grandma, your father and his brother and two sisters used to join him, filling the farmhouse with the sound of music. On weekends and holidays, people from all around would come to hear them play, or join in. Sometimes they toured around through villages and towns playing their music to anybody who cared to listen."

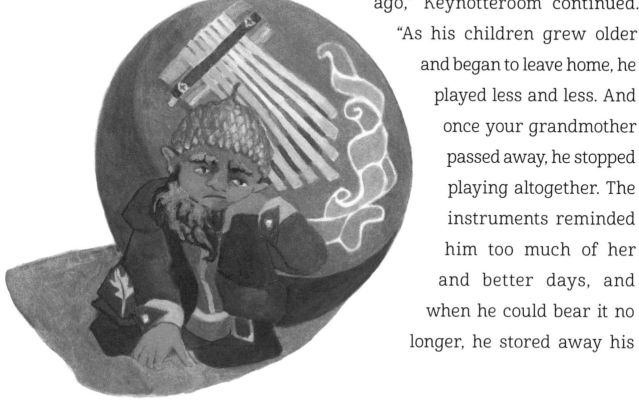

"But alas, that was many, many years ago," Keynotteroom continued. "As his children grew older and began to leave home, he played less and less. And once your grandmother passed away, he stopped playing altogether. The instruments reminded him too much of her and better days, and when he could bear it no longer, he stored away his whole collection up here. Music has not been heard on this farm since that day." Keynotteroom looked glum.

"And that is why we are so unhappy," Flinley said.

"And worst of all, he hasn't laughed in years." As Keynotteroom said those words he shrunk in size, holding his head in his bony hands. Gracie had noticed that Grandpa often looked sad, though he cheered up whenever she talked to him. But she had to admit that she'd never heard him laugh. "I wish he would play his instruments again. I love music. And I want him to be happy again. Really happy."

"And so do all of us tiny folk who live on, in, and around the farm."

Keynotteroom let out a long groan and leaned back against a marimba. "Music has died in our world."

"I will find a way," Gracie declared, banging on a large kettle drum with determination, which startled a pigeon from her nest. "I just don't know how."

"Wait for an opportunity, and it will come," Keynotteroom said, growing slightly taller with hope.

Flinley flew toward the door. "But now it is time to go back, Gracie. Your grandfather might be wondering what has happened to you, and we don't want him to worry." Gracie nodded, though she longed to keep looking around. There were still so many more instruments stored in boxes, baskets, on windowsills, in drawers, dark corners, or hidden behind grimy partitions. On the way out, Gracie spotted a tin whistle lying in the dust by the door. She picked up the little flute and slipped it into her coat pocket. Locking the door and bidding farewell to Keynotteroom they returned to the house.

As soon as they entered the living room of the old farmhouse, Flinley flew toward the gently moving mobile and entered the tin figure of himself.

"Ah, there you are." Grandpa sat in his rocking chair, reading. Tipsy, the cat, jumped onto his lap, purring. "I'll make some lentil soup and we can eat." As he got up with a groan Gracie took out the tin whistle and started to play. "Where did you get that from?" he asked after listening to her play.

"I found it in the hayloft where you keep all your instruments."

"How do you know about my instruments?"

"Flinley, the elf, and Keynotteroom, keeper of the keys, showed me the hayloft."

Grandpa scratched his big grey-white beard. "Ah, I see. Well, they should know. They've witnessed and heard a lot. I have not seen them in years, but they used to dance to the music we made," and he sighed.

"Can you play for me?" she asked holding the tin whistle up to him.

"Not now... maybe some other time. But come here, Gracie. I'll show you how to hold the whistle properly and where to put your fingers." He placed her tiny fingers correctly over the holes. "Good. You're a fast learner. Now you can practice while I heat up the soup." He went into the kitchen leaving her to play, while Gracie enjoyed her newfound melody, swaying slightly to the rhythm.

During supper Grandpa asked. "You have a birthday next weekend, don't you?" Gracie nodded, though she'd quite forgotten about that day. "Is there anything you wish?"

At that moment Keynotteroom appeared by the window, waving his hands and mouthing the words, "Now! Now! Here's your chance!" She understood at once and knew what to say.

"Yes, I do have one wish."

"Well, what is it?"

"I want to have my party right here with you. And I want Mom and Dad, my uncles and aunts, all my cousins, and my best friends to be here. And, of course, my little brother Percy too."

"We can do that," Grandpa said, and he patted her shoulder. "I will talk to your parents. Is that all you want?"

"No, there is one more thing."

"If I can afford it, you may have it."

"It won't cost you a thing." She smiled up at Grandpa. "I want you to bring out all your instruments and play them for us. And I want everybody to sing, dance, and play along."

Grandpa looked at her in surprise. "All my instruments? Hm, what a strange request, Gracie... but I will see what I can do. But now it's time to do the dishes. You can help me." He got up and walked over to the sink. To herself she thought: *My biggest wish is to see you happy again... to see and hear you laugh.*

The following Saturday, when Gracie arrived, she was greeted with cheers by a room full of people. A multitude of instruments lay all around, gleaming and glistening. Grandpa had taken good care to clean and polish every one of them, even the tiniest bell, chime, or harmonica. Colorful lanterns, streamers, and balloons hung from the ceiling and rafters. Grandpa, his eyes glinting with excitement, took Gracie into his strong arms. "Welcome, birthday child. Say hello to everybody, sit down and open your presents. Then we can eat some cake."

"Can we first play some music, Grandpa?

"Music first?" Grandpa asked. "Before opening your presents?"

"Yes, music first."

Everybody looked at Grandpa, and Grandpa looked back at everybody. He didn't say a word.

"Here, take this. I haven't heard you play the fiddle in years." Gracie's father stepped forward and handed Grandpa his old fiddle and bow. Grandpa took it gingerly into his hands, plucked the strings, tuned it and tightened the bow. Carefully he placed it under his chin, lifted the bow and began to play a slow wistful melody, his fingers finding the notes without fail. Keynotteroom appeared and sat on the windowsill while a host of fairies joined the tin elves around the gently swaying mobile. Nobody noticed the happy gathering of the tiny folk. Then, with a holler and a whoop Grandpa launched into a fast jig, which had everybody clapping, laughing, and up on their feet, dancing.

"And now the pennywhistle," Gracie said, handing him the one she had found.

"Fine," and Gracie saw the faintest flicker of a smile flit across his face. "But everybody must pick up an instrument and join in - whatever you can play, even if it is only a triangle, rattle, or shaker." The smile crept up to his sparkling eyes. Once they'd all chosen their instruments, he stamped his foot four times and broke into a jaunty reel. At the end of that tune Gracie handed him a guitar.

And so it went, from one instrument to the next, from tune to tune, from song to song, with everybody singing, dancing, clapping, or playing along. Gracie hopped, skipped, and shook the tambourine.

"Hey Grandpa, can you play this one?" Gracie's brother Percy asked, wobbling under the weight of a big shiny tuba and placing it with a flop onto his lap.

"Of course, I can." At that moment Gracie's mother stepped in from the kitchen with a large chocolate cake topped with icing, cherries, and six brightly lit candles. At once Grandpa hugged the gleaming tuba to his chest and broke into a birthday song, with everybody joining in.

"Happy birthday, Gracie, and I promise you that this will be the first of many musical evenings to come." He laughed. "But now it's time to blow out the candles and make a wish," which she did with one big puff. Everybody whooped, cheered and clapped, including Keynotteroom, Flinley, and the fairies.

"Now, Gracie," continued Grandpa, "pick out any instrument you want in this room and it will be yours." She could hardly believe Grandpa's words, because she did have a secret wish. She wished for the cello she'd spotted in the loft. She had not seen it yet and she wondered whether Grandpa had brought it down? She looked around the large living room, stepping over and between instruments, until at last, she saw it lying behind the double bass on the couch. "That's what I want, that cello."

"Yours it is, and next time you come I will give you your first lesson. But now, let's open up the rest of the presents and eat and drink." After they had feasted, they continued making music until it was time to go home. There were still many instruments that Grandpa had not yet played, and he went from one to the other, much to the joy of all who couldn't believe that he could play them so well. As they played, Gracie saw Flinley and the other elves and fairies twirling and flitting through the air above them, whilst the rustic gnomes and dwarves led by Keynotteroom danced on the windowsills - though no one, except for Gracie and Grandpa, saw them.

Before going home, Gracie put three shovels of coal into the stove, after which she peered up and smiled at the six tiny tin elves suspended on the freely moving mobile. That night, Gracie slept with her new cello lying safely at the foot of her bed. Music and merriment had returned to the farm, but the hearty laughter of her beloved Grandpa made Gracie the happiest.

The End ☾

Lightning Source UK Ltd.
Milton Keynes UK
UKHW051129230721
387627UK00002B/12